JC the Farm Boy

ISBN 978-1-68526-185-6 (Paperback)
ISBN 978-1-68526-186-3 (Digital)

Covenant Books
11661 Hwy 707
Murrells Inlet, SC 29576
www.covenantbooks.com

JC the Farm Boy

Chore Time

BOOK TWO

REBECCA STAAB

Rising slowly and steadily in the east, the sun wakes up the world. Outside, one by one, the animals awaken and begin to dance around. Inside the house, JC jumps out of bed and runs downstairs. "Good morning, world!" He dashes outside in his shorts and down to the barns. "Good morning, piggies! Good morning, kitties! Good morning, Rufus!"

He squeezes through the door to the chicken coop. Inside the coop, the guineas are screaming, the geese are grumbling, the chickens are squawking, and the ducks are just waddling. JC squats down. He begins telling his little feathered friends about the crazy dreams he had last night. "We were saving the world last night! First, we had to get all the animals to join us fighting against the giant.

The pigs ran around circling his legs and made him dizzy. Then the cows sat on top of him, and the geese talked to him and told him that he was being mean.

"The giant sat up and talked to the geese and said, 'I was just trying to find someone to play with, but everyone ran away.' The geese told him they just didn't understand; he needed to speak up and ask them to play.

"Suddenly the conversation was interrupted by the screams of the guineas, the grumbling of the geese, the chickens squawking, and the ducks waddling.

"The giant smiled, raised his voice, and said, 'Okay, if I just asked to play, they would have?'

"'Yep, all the feathered friends love to play too.' The animals and the giant then played hide-and-seek. The giant had so much fun he came back day after day, and they played from dawn until dusk."

JC smiles as he opens the gate, letting the chickens, ducks, guineas, and geese out.

As his feathered friends wander the yard for the day, he fills their water and cleans their pen. He goes inside and wakes his mom and dad. "Wake up, the day has begun!" His mom smiles, and his dad gets up to start the chores.

JC and his dad go outside and check the pigs; they are running around and chasing each other. They check the feed and see that they need to order more. His dad calls the feed mill and orders two and a half ton and tells them which feeders to put it in. They check the waterers and see everything is full and working well. They walk through the pigs' pen, checking to make sure the pigs are healthy and active. Then they check all the fences for holes so the animals don't get out and get lost. When all the work is done, they look around the farm.

JC and Dad go and eat breakfast, Lucky Charms for JC and cornflakes for Dad. They talk about their to-do list for today. Dad says, "We have to mow the lawn, but before that, we need to pick up the sticks that fell from the wind last night." JC smiles and drinks his milk. He puts the bowl on the counter and runs up to wake his sister and brother. They are less than thrilled but know that it takes everybody to make the farm run smoothly. Mom stays inside and cleans up the breakfast mess. The kids go outside after breakfast and start cleaning up the yard.

Timmy, four years older than JC, gets out the four-wheeler and cart and begins picking up sticks. JC and his sister, Sidney, race for the biggest sticks. They count the sticks and are up to seventy-five when they have a full load. They jump up on the cart, and it turns into a Roman chariot and steed. They ride as fast as lightning,

riding past the great Colosseum and the Theatre of Marcellus, with the Roman soldiers slowly gaining ground. Timmy turns and loses them after passing through the Roman Forum. Rome disappears, and they are back on the farm.

Timmy, Sydney, and JC empty the cart and go back for another load. This time, the sticks are scaly snakes slithering back and forth on the jungle floor. Sidney jumps over two of them and then grabs a cobra, weaving back and forth, dodging the enormous fangs. Timmy jumps off the jeep and snatches two more by the tails just as they are about to strike at his faithful dog, Rufus. He quickly ties them together into a bow. The kids capture the serpents and throw them into the cage. One hundred creepy-crawly snakes captured and taken to a pit for snakes. Before long, they are done picking up sticks.

JC gives Timmy and Sidney high fives, and they ride around on the four-wheeler while Dad mows the lawn. They play taxi while the farm turns into a town. JC catches a ride to the farm store to buy farm supplies. They need food for the poultry and new boots for farmwork. He finishes his shopping and then waves down the taxi again for a ride home. Sydney and Timmy are the drivers; they take turns dropping off their fares as the morning wears on. They transport many different people and even give a ride to their "super dog," Rufus. Time flies as their imagination runs rampant, and before long, it is time for lunch.

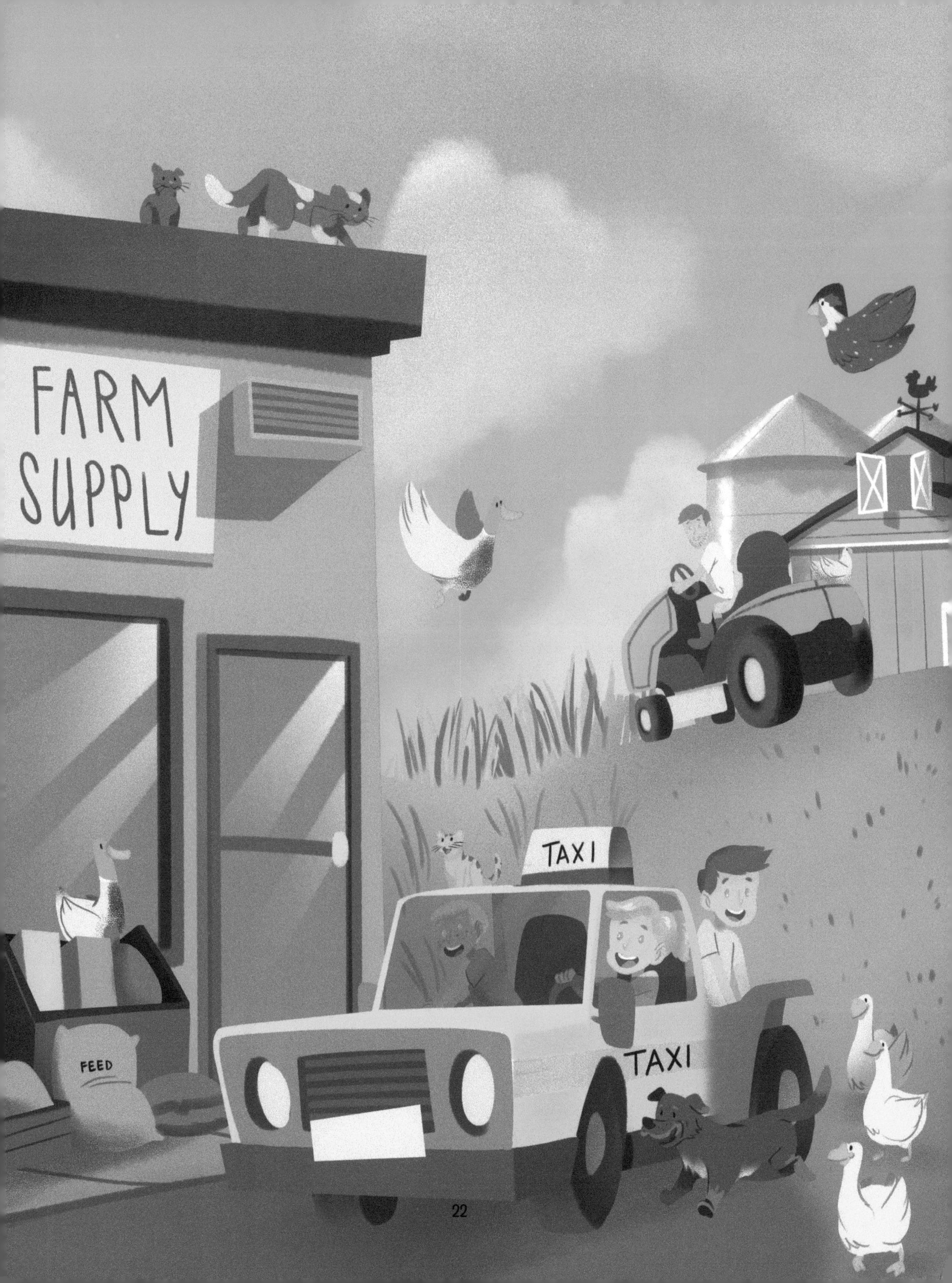
FARM
SUPPLY
TAXI
TAXI
FEED

The kids race inside when Mom calls, and washes their hands. They are all starving!

ABOUT THE AUTHOR

Rebecca works as a registered nurse. Her husband, Donny, and their three children live on an acreage in Northwest Iowa. In her spare time, she loves to read and paint. This is her second book in the series, *JC the Farm Boy*.